THE SEVEN STRIKE GOLD

Enjoy another thrilling adventure with the
Secret Seven. They are Peter, Janet, Pam,
Colin, George, Jack, Barbara and, of
course, Scamper the spaniel.

When Peter discovers a Roman gold coin
while ploughing his father's field, the Secret
Seven determine to investigate further.
Will they find any more Roman remains?
And is the helpful bearded archaeologist
Archibald Davison all that he seems?

The Seven Strike Gold

A new adventure of the
characters created by
Enid Blyton, told by Evelyne
Lallemand, translated by
Anthea Bell

Illustrated by Maureen Bradley

KNIGHT BOOKS
Hodder and Stoughton

Copyright © Librairie Hachette 1979
First published in France as *Les Sept et la déesse d'or*
English language translation copyright © Hodder &
Stoughton Ltd 1984
Illustrations copyright © Hodder & Stoughton Ltd 1984

First published in Great Britain by Knight Books 1984

British Library C.I.P.

Lallemand, Evelyne
  The Seven strike gold.
  I. Title   II. Bradley, Maureen
  III. Les Sept et la déesse d'or. *English*
  843'.914[J]   PZ7

  ISBN 0-340-36391-6

Printed and bound in Great Britain for Hodder and
Stoughton Paperbacks, a division of Hodder and
Stoughton Ltd., Mill Road, Dunton Green, Sevenoaks,
Kent (Editorial Office: 47 Bedford Square, London,
WC1 3DP) by Hunt Barnard Ltd., Aylesbury.

CONTENTS

Chapter One

A THRILLING DISCOVERY

Peter leaned out of his father's tractor for a closer look. Yes – there *was* something shining! Something bright and yellow in the furrow a little way ahead. And Peter had a funny sort of feeling – as if something were going 'Click!' inside his head!

He couldn't help smiling. He knew what *that* meant. It was the feeling he always got when the Secret Seven Society were going to begin a new adventure. He had had it many times before, and it was always a sure sign!

He immediately switched off the tractor engine, jumped down to the ground and ran over to the furrow. He leaned over it, feeling very excited.

The shiny thing was a coin. A metal coin, even if it wasn't quite round and it looked very worn round the edges.

'Dad! Dad!' he shouted. 'Come and see what I've found.'

His father had been working at the other end of the field. He left what he was doing and came striding over to Peter.

'What is it now?' he asked, rather crossly. 'I thought you knew how to drive that tractor! Can't you manage on your own for a few minutes while I mend the fence?'

But then Peter's father suddenly stopped short. He looked at the coin Peter was holding out to him.

'Wherever did you find that?' he asked in amazement.

'Here – in this furrow!' said Peter. 'The plough must have turned it up.'

'Well, I suppose that *must* be what happened,' said

his father. 'It certainly does look a very old coin.'

And he put it in his mouth and bit it!

'Why, it's gold!' he said. 'Real gold!'

Peter's eyes were round with wonder.

'Golly – I bet there are more coins here! Thousands more coins!' he shouted, so loud that several partridges flew up in alarm at the edge of the field.

The Secret Seven held a special meeting in the shed in Peter and Janet's garden. Peter, as their leader, had summoned them. No one was missing – even Scamper the golden spaniel was there, on watch as usual. Everyone in the shed was very excited.

The three girls, Janet, Barbara and Pam, were sitting side by side on some old boxes, chattering away. What could be the reason for this special meeting? Opposite them, George, Jack and Colin were wondering the same thing and suggesting all sorts of ideas. Had Peter invented some wonderful new gadget? Had creatures from outer space landed? It could be anything!

So when Peter got to his feet to tell them what it really *was* all about, the others stopped talking at once. Everything was perfectly quiet as he took the little gold coin out of his pocket. He held it up so that they could all see it shine in the light from the window, and then he passed it round.

'My word – I thought it was chocolate money at first!' whispered Janet when it was her turn to hold it.

She sounded almost disappointed!

'Well, it's gold, sure enough!' breathed Pam. She was very impressed. 'It isn't exactly brand new, either,' she added, turning it over in the palm of her hand.

'I say – there's a pattern or something engraved on it!' said Janet, with interest.

'Good observation, Janet – it's not all that easy to make out,' said Peter. He could see the others were as thrilled by his discovery as he was.

The coin was passed round to George. 'Janet's right,' he said. 'One side of the coin is quite smooth, but the other . . .' And he looked at it more closely. 'The other's embossed.'

'It's a pity we can't see what the picture or pattern was – it's nearly all worn away,' said Jack. He was the last to get a close look at the coin.

'Where exactly did you find it, Peter?' asked Colin. He was beginning to get really interested in Peter's discovery.

'In Broad Acre field,' he told his sister.

'Perhaps there are more coins buried there!' suggested Pam. She was pink in the face with excitement.

'That's exactly what I said to myself, too,' Peter agreed with her. 'And so tomorrow morning the Secret Seven are going digging!'

'Good idea!' said the three boys, jumping up.

'I say – we'll have a real excavating holiday! Just like real archaeologists!' said Barbara, smiling – but *she* was excited too.

'Maybe we'll dig up a pyramid!' said Janet.

Everybody else had been talking nineteen to the dozen, and Scamper had been barking, but they all stopped to laugh at Janet's funny idea! She was a little bit annoyed. What *had* she said that was so comical?

The church clock was striking nine when the bus arrived in the market town next morning. George and Barbara got out and went up to a big double door. It had gold lettering over it saying PUBLIC LIBRARY.

The two children felt a little timid as they walked in. It was the first time they had been inside the town library. They found themselves in a big, very quiet room. All the walls were lined with bookshelves, and the shelves were full of books. There were only two windows, and they were tall and narrow, so you had to have the electric light on all day long. An old man with spectacles sat at a big desk on a sort of little platform at the end of the room.

'My goodness, it's almost like being in church!' whispered Barbara, as she and George went up to the librarian.

When they reached the platform, George asked, rather shyly, 'I say, sir, we want to look at some books about money, please.'

The old gentleman leaned forward so as to get a better look at the children. He smiled at them.

'Money, eh?' he said. 'Going in for high finance, are you?'

'No,' Barbara explained. 'We mean books about coins.'

'Ah, so you take an interest in numismatics. I congratulate you!' said the old man. He came down off his platform.

'No, sir, I'm afraid we don't!' said George bravely. 'We don't know anything about numo . . . nemo . . . what you said. It's actual coins and coinage that we're interested in.'

'But then your *are* numismatists!' the old man told them as he turned towards the bookshelves. The corners of his mouth were twitching slightly. 'Numismatics means the study of coins and coinage!'

George and Barbara couldn't help uttering an exclamation of surprise. 'My word, does it really?' said Barbara. They'd only just become archaeologists – and now apparently they were numismatists too! Who'd have thought it?

This was really a rather promising start to their adventure!

At the same moment a funny sort of procession was arriving at Broad Acre field. It consisted of Peter, Jack, Colin, Pam and Janet. Their bicycles were loaded up with all sorts of tools and implements. At the Secret Seven's meeting the day before they had decided that they'd all bring anything that might come in useful for digging. Jack had borrowed a spade and a pickaxe from his father, and Colin had been to see a cousin of his who was a builder, and who kindly lent him some trowels and buckets and a wire sifter like a big sieve. Pam had brought some brushes and a pair of pincers – she knew archaeologists needed that sort of thing for the delicate part of their work. And Janet had explored the cupboards of Old Mill House and produced a whole collection of kitchen strainers, pairs of tongs and tweezers, pen-knives and little forks. Finally Peter, who was feeling very optimistic, had brought several boxes with tight-fitting lids to hold anything they might dig up.

'Right! We're ready!' he said with satisfaction. 'So let's get down to work straight away.'

'Show us just where you found the coin,' Colin said. 'We ought to begin there – that's the obvious place to dig.'

Peter knew just where the spot was. He marched off into the middle of the ploughed field, and the other children picked up their tools and began digging away with enthusiasm.

Would they find anything else? And if so, what would it be?

Chapter Two

SUSIE BARGES IN

The public library wasn't very busy at this time of year. In the middle of the summer holidays, most people wanted to be out of doors! So the kind old librarian had time to help George and Barbara. He looked at a big book about numismatics, where it told you how to make the design on a coin reappear even if it was almost worn away. All you had to do was put a thin piece of paper over the coin and rub a well sharpened pencil over it, and then the design would appear on the paper. The book said that coin collectors often used this method.

It sounded quite exciting, and George sat down to try. Sure enough, a design *did* come into view as he rubbed his pencil over the paper.

'It's a sort of fork,' said Barbara.

'A fork with three prongs,' agreed George.

'A trident, strictly speaking,' the librarian told them. He adjusted his spectacles and looked more closely at the design. 'We'll have to check it in the books,' he said, 'but I'm almost sure this is a Roman coin.'

'Golly!' said Barbara. 'A *Roman* coin? How exciting!' But suddenly she stopped short, looking thoughtful. 'We're an awfully long way from Italy here, though, aren't we?' she said. 'How could a Roman coin have got into Peter's father's field?'

'Yes, how?' asked George.

'Well, we'll have to go into a little bit of ancient history to explain that!' said the old librarian. He sat down at one of the desks, with the children, and began telling them about the invasion of Britain by the ancient Romans. 'It was about two thousand years ago!' he said. 'First of all Julius Caesar came over from Gaul, which is now France — he had conquered that country already, and made it part of the Roman Empire. Then other Roman leaders came and defeated the ancient Britons. So most of *this* country became part of the Roman Empire too, and was one of its provinces for several hundred years. Roman soldiers may have marched across that field where your friend found this coin, or pitched camp there before a battle. Or a family of Roman settlers may have come to live somewhere near by. In any case, Roman coins hundreds and hundreds of years old have been dug up before in many parts of the country, and now you can see how they got here!'

The two children were fascinated by what the librarian said, and couldn't wait to tell the others what they'd learned.

The sun was rising higher and it was getting warm. As the five children dug away in Broad Acre field, Colin's pickaxe suddenly hit something that made a metallic sound underground! They all stopped as soon as they heard it.

'I say — there certainly is *something* down here!' cried Colin excitedly.

'Go very carefully,' Peter warned him, coming over.

'Use a trowel,' suggested Jack.

But Peter was kneeling down at the spot where the pickaxe had struck. 'It can't be very far down,' he said. 'Better to use hands, I think.'

He was already digging carefully into the soil with his hands, making a little funnel-shaped hole.

'Oh, do be careful!' said Janet.

Just then, before her very eyes, Peter uncovered a little bowl made of some kind of grey metal.

'Oh, how marvellous!' said Pam, gazing at it.

'Look – it's got handles shaped like fish,' said Colin. 'I think it may be a sort of drinking cup.'

'What a pity George and Barbara aren't here,' sighed Jack.

Ever since they arrived at the field, Scamper had been having a lovely time chasing about in the grass and bushes round the sides of it and putting up partridges. But now he suddenly started to bark.

'Listen to old Scamper!' said Jack, smiling. 'He wants to congratulate us on our find!'

But up at the far end of the field Scamper went on barking louder than ever.

'No – I don't think *that's* what he's interested in,' said Peter. 'I'm sure he's picked up the scent of something else. Let's go and look!'

'I'll stay here to guard our treasure!' said Janet, as the others ran over to Scamper.

It didn't take them long to reach the end of the ploughed field, but at first they couldn't see why Scamper was in such a state.

'I can't see anything,' said Pam.

'No – only a field of lucerne the other side of the hedge,' said Jack.

But Scamper was still barking away – and suddenly he pushed his way through the hedge and shot off into the tall lucerne plants. The four children made their own way through the bushes and followed him. He left a sort of wake behind him as he plunged through the lucerne. And suddenly, who do you think they saw pop up in the middle of the lucerne field?

It was Jack's annoying little sister Susie and her friend Binkie! Those two little pests! Scamper had scared them out of hiding – and they took to their heels and ran for it.

'Spying on us again!' shouted Jack angrily.

It was really infuriating the way the two little girls would keep barging in, poking their noses into what the Secret Seven were doing!

'Yes – this is serious!' said Peter gloomily. 'We simply have to keep what we're doing a secret!'

Once Susie and Binkie had disappeared round the bend in the road, Peter and the others hurried home themselves to put the little drinking cup in safety.

It was nearly lunch-time, and all their digging had given them an appetite! They would go on with their archaeology that afternoon, they decided.

The sun was hotter than ever in the afternoon, and there wasn't a single tree in Broad Acre field to give them any shade! Peter, Jack, Pam, Janet and Colin had been working away at digging the soil, but they had found nothing more in over an hour's work. They were beginning to feel tired and depressed when George and Barbara turned up.

'Still toiling away?' said George jokingly.

Jack wasn't in the mood for jokes. '*We're* not frightened of getting blisters on our hands!' he snapped.

'No,' agreed Pam, looking at *her* hands – the palms were covered with blisters, but she had been so absorbed in the digging that she'd hardly noticed.

'All right, you two, you've been sitting about in the library all morning – what did you find out?' asked Peter.

So George and Barbara told them. 'The coin you found is an ancient Roman one!' said Barbara. 'It dates from the time when most of Britain was occupied by the Romans and was part of their Empire.'

'What's more, there was a Roman settlement near here called Fluvia!' said George.

'Fluvia – what a pretty name!' said Janet.

But just then a voice behind them shouted, 'What are you children doing here!'

It was Peter's father! The Seven saw him standing at the end of the field waving his arms about — and he sounded rather cross.

'Come on, get out of there!' he added. 'Just look what you've been doing to my field! Holes all over the place – as if the moles weren't bad enough! A field that was freshly ploughed only yesterday. Peter, I'd have expected you to know better!'

Peter didn't know what to say. He and the others thought it would be wiser not to answer back! They collected all their tools and other things and hurried away from the middle of the field. That calmed Peter's father down a bit.

'What's the idea?' he said, not quite so crossly. 'Are you by any chance hoping to dig up buried treasure? I'm afraid you'll be disappointed. That coin Peter turned up yesterday must have been one that I dropped as a boy – or even my father, years before. He had quite a good coin collection, and passed it on to me. So the *coin* may be an old one, but you're not at all likely to find any more!'

He turned round and went back to the tractor – it was standing in the lane running beside Broad Acre, and he had spotted the children as he drove it along. He set off again, with Scamper going a little way after him, barking. The good dog didn't like it if anyone spoke crossly to his master Peter.

'I bet he *didn't* drop the coin – or my grandfather either!' said Peter, indignantly.

'No. He doesn't know it's a Roman one,' agreed Colin. 'And the little drinking cup is more proof. I suppose if your father had known about that he'd have said it was part of his little sister's doll's teaset, or something!'

Everybody laughed except Peter.

'Anyway, we know it's a Roman coin, and the drinking cup is almost certainly Roman too,' said Barbara firmly.

'Yes. And the question now is, what are we going to do about them?' asked George.

Chapter Three

MORE ARCHAEOLOGY

'I suppose we'd better tell ... tell ... oh, I don't know who exactly, but the police, or a museum, or something,' said Jack. 'I mean, I don't think it's any good keeping the cup a secret any longer, if that means your father won't let us go on digging in the field, Peter. If the authorities say so he'll *have* to let the digging go on!'

'Yes, but you can bet *we* won't be allowed to go on doing it!' said Peter. 'I vote we don't tell anyone. We'll just carry on as before.'

'Daddy will be furious!' said Janet. 'He'll punish us! He'll forbid the Secret Seven to meet in the garden shed, and make us stay at home, and—'

Poor little Janet! She was almost in tears.

'I tell you what,' said Colin. 'We're just as likely to find something *near* the field as *in* the field – specially seeing we didn't find anything else near the place where Peter dug the coin up, except for that one cup. Why don't we try there?' And he pointed to a little hillock covered with brambles at the other end of the field.

'Yes, why not?' said Jack. 'I mean, a few metres one way or the other isn't going to make all that much difference. Peter's coin came all the way from Rome in the first place!'

'I think that's a good idea, Colin,' said Peter. 'That hillock with the bramble bushes is all part of our land, but it's very stony, and my father's never grown anything there.'

'So he can't mind if we dig it up,' finished Barbara. 'And what's more, since it *is* on your land, there won't be anybody else to come along and disturb or bother us!'

The Seven wasted no more time. They fetched all their tools and took them over to the hillock, where they set to work, feeling quite hopeful again. But it was *very* hard work digging, this time! The hillock was hard and stony. It had been much easier to push spades and trowels into the soft earth of the ploughed field. The children kept scratching themselves on the brambles, and they made slow progress. Soon they decided that spades and picks were no use at all, and they had better use their hands. If they moved some of the bigger stones, there might be softer earth below which they could dig more easily. But only too often they would work away to shift a large stone and find nothing but an even bigger one under it! Anyone would think no human being had set foot here for centuries.

Then something happened which almost put a stop to work for the day. Pam was busy shifting a

large stone when she suddenly saw a long snake dart past her!'

'*Help*!' she screamed, running away towards the road.

Janet and Barbara stopped what they were doing at once, and ran to comfort Pam. Poor Pam was trembling all over!

'I could see its tongue – it was an adder, I'm sure it was!' she kept on saying in a terrified voice.

Meanwhile the four boys slashed and beat at the

bramble bushes to drive out any more snakes that might be lurking there – but none appeared.

'It's all right now,' Peter told the girls. 'Even if it *was* an adder and not a harmless grass snake. You know, snakes are more frightened of us than we are of them!'

But Pam didn't believe him, and she said she wasn't going near those bushes again that day. She stayed in the road, watching her friends from a safe distance.

Then, a little later, Janet and Jack had a stroke of luck. They found another coin, underneath a huge stone. The coin was in quite a good state of preservation, too – *and* it clearly showed the trident pattern! A little later Barbara found a third coin tangled in the roots of the brambles.

It wasn't so hot now, and time was getting on. Soon it would be seven o'clock. Pam, who was still waiting for the others in the road, saw Peter's father coming down the lane in his tractor again. When he reached the road, and saw the children working away among the brambles, he stopped.

'We're not doing any harm here, Dad, honestly!' said Peter, before his father had said a word.

'All right, all right,' said Peter's father. 'But watch out for snakes – there are sometimes adders there!'

Pam was just opening her mouth to tell him she *had* seen a snake, but Colin got in first. 'It's not at all likely there'd be any here now!' he said, smiling. 'Not with all the racket we've been making!'

He didn't want Peter's father to know about Pam's snake, just in case he said they mustn't dig among these brambles either.

Starting the tractor up again, Peter's father asked, 'Any luck this afternoon?' He sounded a bit sarcastic.

'No – nothing at all!' said Jack untruthfully.

Peter's father smiled. 'Well, don't forget to go home. It's nearly supper time for all of you, I'm sure, and it certainly is for Peter and Janet.'

'We're coming,' Peter told him, secretly squeezing the two coins he had put in his pocket.

When the Seven met at their archaeological 'dig' next morning, they had a nasty surprise. Susie and Binkie were there before them. The two little girls were walking up and down the ploughed field with baskets over their arms, eyes on the ground. What were they looking for? Had they guessed what the Seven were up to?'

'Oh no! *Bother*! Those two awful little pests!' said Jack crossly. He couldn't stand the way his sister kept wanting to interfere with what the Seven were doing – and Binkie was just as bad.

'We must get rid of them as quickly as we can,' said Peter. 'We certainly don't want to start digging right under their noses!'

'I've got an idea,' Colin told his friends. 'You just wait!'

He moved away from the others, who had gathered close to the hillock with the bramble bushes, and went over to the two girls in the middle of Broad Acre field.

'Nice weather, isn't it?' he said in a polite tone of voice.

'It's a funny thing, but the moment I see you the sky seems to cloud over!' Binkie answered back.

Susie giggled, but Colin refused to take any notice. He went on, in the same cheerful voice. 'Well, if you're after the same things as *we're* after you won't find many today!'

'Many what?' asked Binkie, falling straight into Colin's trap.

'You *know* what, Binkie! I've told you hundreds of times!' said Susie. *She* guessed that Colin was up to something, and Binkie's question had been a mistake.

'No, you haven't! You never said *exactly*,' Binkie began, but Susie interrupted her.

'Oh, don't be so *silly*! Can't you ever remember anything?'

While the two little girls were quarrelling, Colin crouched down and started digging about in the earth with his fingers. Soon he let out a shout of triumph.

'I say – you *are* in luck after all! I've found one!' he said.

And he waved an enormous worm under Binkie's nose! The little girl tried to hit out at him with her basket, but he ducked and went on waving the worm in her face.

'If you're going fishing, you'll need some bait!' he said teasingly.

'Bait yourself!' said Susie angrily.

'He's *in* a bait himself!' said Binkie, feeling rather proud of this insult – but next moment she ducked and squealed as the worm almost touched her.

'Come on, never mind him,' said Susie, and she marched off, with Binkie after her.

The rest of the Secret Seven congratulated Colin on his clever trick. Even Scamper barked approvingly. The two little girls really had 'risen to the bait', and the Seven agreed that from now on they'd have to call on Colin to deal with them!

And now that the coast was clear they could begin their archaeological work again. To make quite sure nobody disturbed them, Peter put Scamper in the road to keep watch. The spaniel would let them know if anyone came along.

The children had been scratched so often the day before that they had come equipped with boots and gloves this time, and they had borrowed garden secateurs to cut back the brambles. They could work much faster now. Jack and Peter soon cleared quite a large patch of ground, and by lunch-time the whole of the southern side of the hillock had been cleared of brambles and other plants.

They had spent most of the morning just clearing the ground, and now they could begin a proper 'dig' in the afternoon. They had brought some iron bars along to use as levers, and with the aid of these bars they managed to shift some really big rocks. Unfortunately all they found underneath was more stones!

In fact, it was quite late in the afternoon before the Seven *did* find something interesting – a big round stone which didn't look anything like the others. Once they had rubbed off the layer of dried mud on it, they could see the stone was smooth and had a very fine texture. It was a sort of salmon pink colour, too, with pretty amber veins in it.

'I say – I think that's marble!' said Colin. 'We've got some stone that looks very like it round a fireplace at home.'

'If we could only shift it, I'm sure we'd find something!' said Peter. 'This looks like the key to a real find!'

'Let's move away the pebbles and soil around it,' Jack suggested. 'Then we'll be able to tell whether we can lever it right out.'

They were all getting very excited – they'd made no discoveries at all since yesterday, but this looked as if it might be a really important one. All seven of them set to work, and soon they had cleared the ground round the piece of marble. As it came into sight they could see it was even bigger than they had thought at first. It was shaped like a cylinder.

'Oh, look – it's been carved!' cried Janet, pointing to some grooves cut into the stone.

'I think I know what this is! I bet you anything it's a *column*!' said Jack. He was delighted.

'You're right!' agreed Colin happily. 'Come on, let's dig down a bit deeper.'

But the Seven soon found out that their find was only *part* of a column. It had broken off, and was buried there in the ground.

'We'll get it loose and lever it out,' said Peter. 'Come on, everyone, lend a hand!'

They got an iron bar underneath the broken-off column, and began pushing down on it.

'With a *one* – and a *two* – and a *three*!' the girls chanted, to help the boys get a good rhythm going as they worked away at their lever. 'With a *one* – and a *two* – and a *three*!'

At last the piece of marble column wobbled, came up out of the ground, toppled over, and came to rest at the foot of the hillock, on the soft soil of Broad Acre field.

The Seven all clustered round to admire it. All but

George! He knew what *he* was after. He was busy digging in the crumbly soil where the piece of marble had been lying, working feverishly, groping about with his hands – and suddenly he let out a shout of triumph.

When the others turned to look at him, they saw him brandishing a magnificent gold bracelet in the air!

Three coins, a drinking cup, part of a column, and now a bracelet! Could they still keep their finds a secret, or had the time come to tell someone else about them? The Seven couldn't make up their minds – and it wasn't until the end of a rather stormy meeting in the garden shed that evening that they came to a decision.

Chapter Four

AND AN ARCHAEOLOGIST!

When they went up to the Hall next day, however, they were sure they were doing the right thing, for everyone's good. They had decided that Mr Fitzwilliam, who lived at the Hall, was the best person to let into the secret. He had lots of beautiful and valuable things in his big house, and sometimes lent them to museums and exhibitions, so the Seven thought he was likely to know more about antiquities than the other people in the village did.

'I believe the coins and bracelet we've found must be treasure trove!' said Peter. 'And anything else we find would be treasure trove too. That means we've no right to keep it to ourselves. Other people ought to be able to see these Roman things – in a museum or somewhere. Mr Fitzwilliam will know what to do about them.'

Luckily Mr Fitzwilliam was at home, and was happy to see the children, who were old friends of his. 'Well, and what have you young people come about?' he asked, inviting them into his study.

Without a word, Peter put a little black bag down on Mr Fitzwilliam's desk. Mr Fitzwilliam opened it – and his jaw dropped in astonishment.

'Magnificent!' he breathed at last, after several moments' silence. He was gazing at the bracelet and the cup. 'Where do they come from?'

'Broad Acre Field, sir!' said Peter, and he told Mr Fitzwilliam all about it.

Mr Fitzwilliam got quite excited. He told the Seven they had been right to come to him, and he rang up the local newspaper. Next day there was an article in it all about the discoveries the Seven had made, with photographs of the coins, the cup and the bracelet.

Peter's father was quite impressed! He had been quite sure that the children wouldn't find anything after that first coin, but he had to admit he'd been wrong. He even said they could dig in Broad Acre field again – although he was none too pleased when he found that other people had had the same idea and were digging there *without* his permission. But a word with the Inspector at the police station soon dealt with that problem, and the Seven were able to go on with their archaeology in the field and on the hillock undisturbed.

However, they didn't find very much more. A few more coins came to light, but that was all. And then, one day, the children arrived at Broad Acre field to find a Landrover parked by the side of the road. A

moment or so later they saw that a man in a safari suit and a sun-hat was on the site of their dig, busy looking underneath some stones.

He straightened up when he saw them coming. 'How do you do, young people? My name is Archibald Davison,' he told them.

'What are you doing here?' asked Peter, scowling.

'I've come to lend a hand!' said the man, smiling through the thick black beard which covered most of his face. 'And you're in luck. I just happened to be passing through this part of the country when I saw the story about you in the newspaper, and decided it would be worth staying!'

'We don't want anyone to lend us a hand!' said Jack. He didn't think much of this interfering man. 'The land where the things were found belongs to Peter's father, and you need his permission to be on it.'

'Yes – and Daddy said *we* could do all the digging, and he wouldn't let other people bother us,' said Janet firmly.

'So I'm afraid that if you wanted to dig here, you're *not* in luck, sir,' added Colin, just as firmly.

'Well, well – what enterprising children you are!' said the man, in a sugary sort of voice. 'I'm sure your hearts are in the right place, but the fact is, you won't get very far without someone more experienced to help. You take my word for it!'

That was the last thing the Seven felt like doing! They looked angrily at the man.

'My name may not mean anything to *you*,' he went on, 'but it happens to be quite well known in the rest of the world! I'm an archaeologist, you see, and I've travelled very widely. I've worked in Egypt, Greece, Peru, on the Amazon—'

'Never mind that! We don't want you working *here*!' snapped Peter. He had stepped forward and was face to face with the archaeologist. He had gone rather pale, and the faithful Scamper, sticking close to him, was growling.

'Now you listen to me, young man!' Mr Davison went on. 'I'll admit that you *have* been lucky so far. In fact it's little short of a miracle that you've managed to get your finds out of the ground intact. What you don't realise is that there are all sorts of complex but reliable techniques for archaeological work of this sort. If you carry on alone in your amateurish way you're heading for disaster.'

'Please go *away*!' said Peter, through his teeth.

'Just as you like,' said the man, with a mocking smile. And he made for the gateway into the field. Just as he was turning into the lane, however, he looked back and called, 'Oh, if you ever change your minds, you'll find me staying at the Manor House Hotel. I'll be seeing you soon – I expect!'

He climbed into his Landrover and started off, with a last sarcastic smile.

'What a cheek!' said Peter furiously. 'Even if he was the Duke of Edinburgh or somebody, he's got no right just to march on to someone's private property.'

'Yes – the Secret Seven and nobody else are doing the digging here!' said Jack, backing his friend up. 'Your father said that was all right – and what's more, so did Mr Fitzwilliam!'

'You don't have to be grown-up and tremendously clever to move stones about!' agreed Barbara. 'Or to have travelled to Egypt and Peru and those other places!'

'Barbara's right,' said Pam. 'We don't want any outsiders barging in – this is *our* adventure.'

But while the nosy archaeologist had thoroughly annoyed all the others, George seemed very thoughtful. He was standing there in silence, and it was a long time before he said anything. Then he muttered, 'Davison . . . Archibald Davison. I'm sure I've heard that name before, somewhere. But where?'

He couldn't answer his own question, and the Seven set to work again. Hours passed by, and yet again, as on several days before, they found nothing at all.

Something quite dramatic was soon to happen, though! Janet was busy digging carefully away when she found something, and called to Jack, who was nearest to her.

'Jack, come and look! There, at the bottom of my trench!'

Jack came over and, like Janet, he saw a piece of pottery sticking up out of the ground. He leaned over it and carefully cleared away more soil all round it with his trowel.

'I think it's the handle of a vase!' he said. 'And look – there are the remains of some painting on it!'

The rest of the Secret Seven came along to help with getting the vase out. Now that it was almost uncovered they could see that it was a really magnificent one. There were pictures of beautiful women with almond-shaped eyes on its sides.

At last the children had almost dug it out, and Jack and Janet each took one of its handles to lift it up, out of the earth that had been surrounding it for centuries. But oh dear! Did they jerk the vase too suddenly? Was it too heavy? Anyway, whatever the reason, the result was that as they lifted the vase it broke into three pieces.

'Archibald Davison!' said George suddenly. '*Now* I know! I saw his name on a whole lot of books in the Public Library! He'd written them. They even had his photograph on them too.'

'I'm afraid we're going to need him after all,' said Peter gloomily, staring at the remains of the old vase.

It wasn't an easy decision for the Secret Seven to take. None of them had really liked the archaeologist, and when they met in the garden shed that afternoon they spent a long time discussing things. Some of the children wanted to go on with their digging by themselves, while others thought it would be more sensible to ask for help. Peter had liked Mr Davison least of all, but he was a very just boy, and *he* thought they ought to go and see him.

George went into the town by bus, and came back in the evening with several books by the archaeologist which he had borrowed from the library. Now everyone could see his photograph on the covers of the books – and when they had looked inside the books themselves, they had to admit that they couldn't ask for anyone better qualified to advise them.

'It's a funny thing,' said Colin, 'he looks rather younger now than he does in that photograph – and the date under it says it was taken five years ago!'

'That's not surprising,' said Barbara. 'After all, the photo was taken out in the Egyptian desert, and I expect Mr Davison was feeling the effects of the heat. He looks as if he were really exhausted with all his work, and that makes him seem older.'

Once the Seven had made their decision, they looked at the time. It was not too late to go and call on Mr Davison. They warned their parents they might be late for supper, and then they set off on their bicycles for the Manor House Hotel, out along a country road about a short bike-ride away.

As soon as they arrived, they saw the Landrover parked outside the hotel. A few moments later they were walking down a long corridor with a red carpet, and then Peter knocked at the door of Room 212, where the archaeologist was staying.

Chapter Five

PROFESSIONAL ADVICE

The digging got going again, but this time with Mr Davison in charge. Now that the Seven had his professional advice things seemed different, and much more official.

The archaeologist started by clearing the entire hillock of brushwood and brambles, so that he could get a better idea of the work that would have to be done. Then he told the children how to mark out the ground in rectangles, using pegs and string. Barbara drew a plan of the site, marking each square with a number. Anything they dug up could now be labelled to show the exact place where it had been found.

This method meant that they could work faster and more safely. And Mr Davison had lots of archaeological tools which he let the Seven use. As they were made especially for the job of archaeological excavation, they turned out to be very useful indeed.

The vase which Jack and Janet had found was lying beside some stones set side by side, and it turned out that they were really a little wall. The two children went on uncovering it, using brushes and fine spatulas so as not to damage anything. Meanwhile Peter, Jack and Pam were probing the ground with long metal rods. As for George and Barbara, they had made the exciting discovery of another column, and they and Mr Davison were busy digging it out of the ground.

And the new method of working soon had spectacular results!

Less than two days after the archaeologist had started directing operations, Peter dug up a magnificent sword with a beautifully engraved bronze hilt, and Pam had a great stroke of luck when she found a golden necklace. Jack found several more coins, and Barbara dug up a second bracelet, set with rubies this time. Then there was a wonderful, big, solid silver dish, dug up by Mr Davison himself.

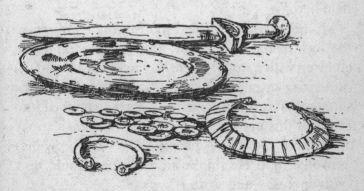

Every evening the Seven went up to the Hall, to leave the things they had found with Mr Fitzwilliam, who had a safe in the house where he could lock them up.

After only a week, they had found about sixty separate items in or near Broad Acre field! And Peter had a good idea.

'Mr Fitzwilliam,' he said when they arrived at the Hall that evening to leave their treasures in the safe, 'we've got something to ask you.'

'Let's hear it, then!' said Mr Fitzwilliam, smiling. 'I don't expect I'll say no.'

'It's like this,' said Jack. 'We thought all the people who live near here ought to be able to see these interesting Roman things.'

'A very good idea,' said Mr Fitzwilliam. He put the bag containing that day's finds in his safe, and locked it up.

'We were thinking of an exhibition,' said Pam. 'An exhibition here at the Hall – that is, if you'd let it be held here?'

Mr Fitzwilliam finished moving the numbers on the lock of the safe round, and then turned to the children with a smile. 'Well, do you know, I'd had the same idea myself!' he said. 'You really are making some remarkable discoveries! I even mentioned it to Davison this morning. You know, it's quite a stroke of luck for you young people to be working with a man like that! He thinks an exhibition would be a great success – and so do I!'

'Oh, thank you!' cried the Seven. They were delighted!

'What about using the Gallery as the exhibition room?' Mr Fitzwilliam went on.

'Oh yes, what a good idea!' said George. 'That would be the perfect place!'

The others all nodded. The Gallery was a big, long room, with pictures of Mr Fitzwilliam's ancestors hanging on the walls, but without much furniture in it. It would be ideal for an exhibition.

'And I know someone who'd be happy to help organise it – Mr Roberts, the librarian from the town Public Library!'

'Oh, good!' said Barbara. She had grown very fond of the old man.

'But we must make sure we've dug up everything there *is* to dig up, before we fix a date for the exhibition,' Peter said.

'And at the moment it looks as if we'll still be digging things up right to the end of the holidays,' added Colin.

'We're having a real excavating holiday, just as I said we would!' finished Barbara happily.

The Seven worked away as hard as they could. They made several more discoveries – and then quite suddenly, after three weeks, it seemed there was nothing more at all to be found.

Jack and Janet had uncovered the little wall. It turned out to be shaped like a horseshoe, and Mr Davison said that showed that it had been part of a small country temple to a Roman nature god.

They went on digging inside and outside the wall for several days, but they didn't find anything. Not a coin, not so much as a scrap of pottery. It looked as if the dig was exhausted.

But Mr Davison insisted that there must be more to find, and even when the Seven felt too discouraged to do any more and put their tools down, he went on digging by himself.

'A true archaeologist never admits that he is beaten!' he said, hacking away with a pickaxe. 'Good heavens, if I'd stopped the digging all those years ago in Peru, just because I wasn't finding anything, I'd never have dug up the statue of Apollo! I remember it so well – my site was on the banks of a lake, and I'd been digging in vain for over three months, when suddenly, one fine morning, I saw a hand literally reaching out to me from the ground!'

The Seven felt impressed. What a great moment that must have been!

'Tell us more about your digs!' said Pam, admiringly.

'Yes – where else have you been?' asked George.

'Did you ever work in Egypt?' asked Colin.

Peter pricked up his ears. Why was his friend asking the archaeologist if he'd been to Egypt, when they'd all seen that photograph of Mr Davison busy excavating in the desert?

'Egypt! Indeed I've worked there!' said Archibald Davison. 'I was there for ten years. I was in charge of the excavations at Alexandria – you should have seen them! All those mummies and sphinxes and pyramids! In fact I've written several books on the subject.'

'Oh, I know!' said Janet proudly. 'We've read them!'

Mr Davison swung round and looked at the Seven – almost as if he were worried! 'You . . . you say you've read them?' he repeated.

'Well, just leafed through them, really,' Jack admitted. 'They're rather too learned and clever for us, sir.'

'Yes, naturally,' said the archaeologist, nodding, and he ran his hand rather nervously over his beard. Then he went back to his work.

It was hot in the garden shed that afternoon. The weather was very fine, and it was the middle of August. Scamper was lying on the floor panting, with his tongue out. He watched lazily as Colin paced up and down the shed, talking excitedly to his surprised friends.

'I tell you, he isn't Archibald Davison at all!' Colin was saying. He was so hot and excited that he was perspiring. 'What's more, I can *prove* it! In fact I've got *three* proofs! First there's that photograph. He looks older in the photograph than in real life, which just isn't possible, seeing the photo was taken more than five years ago.'

'But he *was* tired out,' Barbara began, 'so we can't be sure that—'

'And the second proof,' Colin interrupted her impatiently, 'is what he said about a statue of Apollo in Peru. I mean, everybody knows Apollo was a *Greek* god!'

'You're right!' said Peter, with a low whistle of surprise. 'He did say he was working in Peru when he found a statue of Apollo!'

'Yes – though I didn't actually notice how odd it was when he first mentioned it,' said Pam. 'What he said about the hand reaching out to him was so dramatic, I didn't realise it was odd about Apollo!'

'And the third proof,' Colin went on, still pacing up and down the shed, 'is what he said about the excavations at Alexandria!'

'But Alexandria exists all right!' Janet protested. 'We learned about it in geography at school. It's a seaport on the Mediterranean. You can't say—'

'Oh, it exists, sure enough!' said Colin. 'Only Alexandria hadn't even been built in the time of the Pharoahs who were buried in pyramids! It was built much later, by King Alexander the Great of Macedon. And there were never any mummies or pyramids there at all!'

He stopped and looked at the others.

'Do you honestly think an archaeologist with a world-wide reputation would make simple mistakes like that?' he said.

'No, certainly not!' said George, impressed by Colin's arguments.

'But who *is* he if he isn't really Archibald Davison?' asked Barbara anxiously.

'He may be the real Archibald Davison after all,'

suggested Pam. 'Colin's proofs don't tell us anything for sure. Take the photograph: you can't be certain exactly how many wrinkles he's got under all that beard! And as for his . . . well . . . geographical mistakes – you know how famous professors are for being absent-minded! I read something in a magazine which said the greatest brains are capable of making the simplest of mistakes.'

'Yes, that's true,' agreed Peter. 'Your proofs aren't definite evidence, Colin.'

Colin looked cross! He was going to answer back, but Peter raised one hand for silence.

'All the same, they *are* worrying,' the leader of the Secret Seven went on. 'What I suggest is that we all keep an eye on Mr Davison – and we keep it wide open, too! But we don't know anything against him for sure.'

'Listen, did *you* like him when you first saw him, all of you?' asked Colin angrily. 'I tell you he's an impostor – and he means no good!'

Scamper grunted, and fell asleep, worn out by the heat. *He* didn't mind one way or the other.

It was a different matter for the Secret Seven themselves!

Chapter Six

THE GODDESS FLUVIA

The Seven went back to their digging with enthusiasm next day. It wasn't so much that they hoped to make any more discoveries as that they wanted to watch the archaeologist. They never took their eyes off him for a moment. Even at lunch-time one or other of them managed to follow him back to the Manor House Hotel, where he ate his meals, and Peter made sure *he* was always the last to leave the site in the evenings.

However, even if Archibald Davison really was an impostor, as Colin claimed, was he at all dangerous to them at the moment? They weren't digging anything up at present, and they hadn't found anything of value for days. The only new discovery had been a marble slab they had unearthed inside the horseshoe shape of the temple wall. It was obviously part of the temple floor, and there wasn't much chance of anything else being buried underneath it. But the archaeologist insisted on going on with the work.

One night, when Jack and his mother and father had been out to see some friends and were passing

Broad Acre on their way home in the dark, he saw Mr
Davison back on the site again, digging away by the
light of a lantern. What could he be looking for?

It wasn't long before the Seven were able to make a
good guess!

One day when they went to the library to visit Mr
Roberts and talk about the exhibition, George,
Barbara and Colin found that he had just got a new
book – in fact he had sent for it especially so that they
could read it. It was all about Roman Britain, and it
looked very interesting. They leafed through it at
once, and stopped to read about Fluvia, the Roman
name for their own part of the country. Apparently it
was called after a Romano-British goddess whose
name was Fluvia. The children read on, and held
their breath when they came to the next paragraph.

'I say – listen to *this*!' said Colin, reading aloud.

' "A rich Roman settler, who believed the goddess had brought good luck to his fields and flocks, is said to have had a statue made in her honour. This statue was solid gold, covered with diamonds." '

'My word! So *that's* what Mr Davison is looking for!' cried George. 'He hopes to find the statue of Fluvia – and obviously he isn't planning to put it in the exhibition, because he hasn't breathed a word about it to us!'

'Wait a minute!' said Barbara. She too was reading on. 'Listen to the next bit. "Said to be of priceless value, the statue of Fluvia has never been found, and some eminent archaeologists believe that the story of its existence is no more than a legend passed down by popular tradition." '

'That doesn't make any difference,' said Colin. 'Whether the statue really exists or not, Mr Davison is after it. And if the story *is* true . . .'

He stopped. It would be a tremendously important discovery – so important he could hardly take it in! Barbara and George were watching him, their eyes shining with excitement.

Mr Roberts hadn't been able to follow the whole of their conversation, but he could see how thrilled they were, and tried to bring them down to earth.

'I wouldn't get too excited, children,' he said. 'If there was any real chance of finding that statue buried near here, we'd have had people coming from all over the world to look for it years and years ago. So don't be too hopeful!'

Of course what Mr Roberts said was very sensible, but all the same, the Seven dug away with more enthusiasm than ever over the next few days. Archibald Davison was digging frantically too. He hardly said anything to the children; he just smoked cigarette after cigarette. Peter tried to persuade him to give up work, several times.

'We're not going to find anything else now,' he told the archaeologist. 'You could quite well go home – I'm sure this site is exhausted.'

But whenever Peter mentioned the subject, Archibald Davison produced some new excuse for staying on. And when Colin asked why he was so keen to go on digging, he always said, 'You never know – you never know!' Then he dug away harder than before!

Time went by. September came, and the first of the autumn mists. The days were shorter now, and the mornings and evenings were cooler. Soon the summer holidays would be coming to an end.

It was on a Monday morning that Janet made the wonderful discovery. You wouldn't have known it *was* a wonderful one at first, since she let out a shrill scream. Anyone would have thought that, like Pam, she'd been frightened by a snake.

She had just brushed the earth away from a face! The face of a beautiful woman, and made of solid gold! It must be the goddess Fluvia.

Janet fell to her knees. She was so excited that she

was crying — but she was laughing through her tears too.

Everyone else came running up. There were shouts and exclamations, and a few more tears. Archibald Davison was on his knees too, looking at the lovely golden face set with diamonds. However, he said nothing, and if *he* was pleased he didn't show it. After a few moments, however, when the first shock of the surprise had worn off he remarked, in a chilly sort of voice, 'Well, you see, I was right to go on digging.'

And that was all he said about Fluvia! It was just as if he didn't want to let the Seven know what a very important discovery they had made.

The children were even more watchful now. They must get the statue out of the ground and locked up safely in Mr Fitzwilliam's house as soon as they possibly could.

But they were not in luck. It was much more difficult than they had expected to dig the statue out. Fluvia was wedged tight by two heavy marble slabs close to her neck. None of the childen's levers, or the equipment Mr Davison had brought, could shift the slabs at all, and when evening came the goddess was still imprisoned. The diamonds on her forehead sparkled with pink light in the rays of the setting sun.

The Seven waited until at last Mr Davison left before covering her face with a scarf and sprinkling a few handfuls of earth over it to hide it. Now nobody could tell what a treasure there was here in the middle of the fields!

Overnight the weather changed. Big black clouds piled up in the sky, and a storm broke. When the Seven woke up next morning they had a nasty surprise. It was simply pouring with rain!

All the same, they met at the site of their excavation as usual. They waited patiently, wearing raincoats with the hoods up, and hoping the rain would stop. They couldn't take their eyes off the little heap of earth in the middle of the site. The goddess Fluvia lay under it!

It was raining as hard as ever at lunch-time, and Archibald Davison still hadn't turned up. Peter decided that he and Jack would go and see the archaeologist while the others went on standing guard.

When they reached the Manor House Hotel, the two boys went up to Mr Davison's room. They knew the way to go because they had been to the hotel before. He was in, and was calmly reading the newspaper.

'Hallo, and what brings you two here?' he asked.

'We wondered why you hadn't come to the site to go on working,' said Peter.

'Oh, well, it wouldn't be any good working in weather like this,' said Mr Davison. 'The ground is too slippery in the rain, you see, and we'd risk damaging the statue.'

'Yes, I see,' said Peter. 'Well, some of us are on guard at the moment, and we'll stay there until the sun comes out again!'

He had spoken in a way that made Archibald Davison put his paper down and look at him. Did the archaeologist notice the threat in his voice? He hadn't been able to keep it out, although he had meant to. There was an awkward silence as all three people in the room looked at each other suspiciously.

'Why don't you spend a rainy day like this getting your exhibition ready?' asked Archibald Davison. 'That would be of more use.' He was obviously trying rather hard to sound casual.

'We did think of that,' Jack told him. 'And we're going up to the Hall now!'

'But that needn't stop us leaving one or two people to watch the site!' said Peter, as they left.

Colin was the first to be on guard. He got very cold, and he was soaked through – there was so much rain it even got through his raincoat! But he stayed at his post until darkness fell, keeping watch over Fluvia.

Next day it was *still* raining – what a nuisance! Jack said he would be on guard this time.

The rest of the Seven were busy up at the Hall. With the help of Mr Roberts, they were turning the Gallery into an exhibition room. There were some shelves with a collection of china on them. Barbara and Janet cleared Mr Fitzwilliam's china carefully away, and put out the things they had been digging up on the archaeological site over the last few weeks. Pam wrote labels, saying on what date each item had been found, and exactly where on the big plan of the site that George was drawing up. Peter and Colin explored the attics of the Hall and found some big wooden stands like pedestals. They would come in useful for displaying the best of the exhibits. All they needed was a new coat of white paint, and then they looked very smart indeed!

Nice and warm indoors, and absorbed in the fascinating work of getting the exhibition ready, the Seven didn't even hear the rain, which was still beating against the windows of the Gallery as gusts of wind blew it against the glass.

Poor Jack noticed it all right, though! Standing there doggedly in Broad Acre field, he could feel himself beginning to catch a cold.

When Peter opened his eyes next morning he saw sunlight coming in at his bedroom window.

'Hurrah!' he thought. 'We'll be able to take Fluvia up to the Hall today.' And he jumped out of bed to get washed and dressed and ready to go out.

Once he and the others reached the site of the excavations, however, their cheerful mood soon wore off. All the rain that had fallen over the last few days had turned the site into a sea of mud. And the children were very sorry to see that part of the temple wall they had dug out had collapsed. It was going to be quite hard to find the exact place again where the statue lay hidden!

Archibald Davison had turned up too, and he didn't try to hide the fact that he was very worried.

'The ground is very soft,' he said. 'I'm afraid parts

of the temple remains have slipped out of position.'

'Well, it's not the first time there's been a heavy rainstorm in Broad Acre field!' Jack pointed out.

'No – but you see, the stones we moved before we began digging were acting as a sort of protective layer over the temple,' the archaeologist explained. 'And all the brambles that grew on the hillock helped to hold back the water.'

'We'd better start shifting the mud!' said Peter. 'We have spades here, and buckets, so let's get to work!'

It wasn't as much fun as digging with buckets and spades at the seaside, and it took the Seven and the archaeologist the whole morning to find Fluvia again. But at last they did. The little golden statue was still there, safe under Pam's scarf, with her shining face turned up to the blue sky.

The rain might have delayed their work, but it made things easier once they *could* begin again. The marble slabs lying close to the statue had moved quite a bit once the rain had softened the ground around them, and the Seven could easily get their levers further into the earth than before. After an hour and a half of careful work, Fluvia came right out into the light of day!

Once they had washed the statue in clean water, they could see her in all her glory. She was about forty centimetres tall, and made of solid gold, just as the legend said. And over twenty diamonds sparkled on her forehead, her neck, and the hem of her robes!

The Seven surrounded their find and admired her for a few minutes in silence. Even Scamper seemed to be impressed! He wagged his tail and panted like anything – he was fascinated by the sparkle of the diamonds. As for Archibald Davison, the children had never seen him smile so happily before. You could see it even through his beard!

A little later, once they had pulled themselves together again, the Seven set off to take the statue up to the Hall. They wanted to make sure Fluvia was in safety.

Chapter Seven

THE EXHIBITION

The Seven were very busy all next week with preparations for the exhibition. There were posters up advertising it all over the neighbouring towns and villages.

The children didn't see much of Archibald Davison. He came up to the Hall once or twice, but he didn't give advice unless he was asked for it, and kept quiet the rest of the time, hiding behind his beard, as Mr Fitzwilliam said. Mr Fitzwilliam had been very friendly to him, but the archaeologist was rather gruff in return. He didn't even seem to want to be there on the day the exhibition was opened, but Mr Fitzwilliam insisted he must stay for the great occasion. None of this really surprised the Seven. They had never taken to Archibald Davison, from the start. However, they didn't really believe he was an impostor any more. He had been a lot of help in their excavations, and he'd never tried to hide something he had found from the rest of them. No, he was just an absent-minded professor sort of person with a rather prickly character, the children decided!

Everything was ready up at the Hall when another violent storm broke, two nights before the exhibition was to open. The rolls of thunder and flashes of lightning must have woken everyone for miles around. There were such large hailstones that one motorist's windscreen was broken. The wind tore branches off trees, and water flowed down the roads and overflowed the gutters, flooding several cellars in the village. Nobody had known a storm like it for more than twenty-five years.

First thing next morning the Seven went up to the Hall. They were alarmed to see all the damage the storm had done, with branches and leaves lying all over the drive. Once they reached the house, they went straight to the Gallery. They weren't really surprised to find that the panes of one window had been broken by the strong wind during the night. Luckily none of the exhibits had been damaged, and Fluvia was standing on pedestal in the very middle of the long room, just where they had left her.

They went to find Mr Fitzwilliam and tell him about the damage to his window, and he sent for a workman to come and put new glass into it. Then they swept up the broken bits of the old panes, dusted the shelves, and made sure everything was ready for the exhibition.

It was opened at eleven o'clock next morning – a Saturday, so lots of people were able to come. There was quite a crowd in the Gallery at the Hall.

First of all, Mr Fitzwilliam welcomed the parents of the Seven, and congratulated them on having such clever and hard-working children. Then he went round shaking hands with other people. It looked as if almost everyone the Seven knew had come – and quite a few people they didn't know, too. Several of the visitors were tourists on holiday in the area, and thought that an exhibition of newly discovered archaeological items from Roman Britain sounded very interesting. They asked to be introduced to the Seven too, and exclaimed in surprise when they heard the story of their discoveries.

Then Mr Fitzwilliam looked round for Archibald Davison – he wanted to introduce *him* to the people who had come to see the exhibition, too. But the archaeologist was nowhere to be seen!

'Here he comes!' whispered Pam, pointing to the doorway, where Mr Roberts was handing out some leaflets that had been printed, saying what the exhibits were.

'And here,' said Mr Fitzwilliam, shaking Mr Davison's hand, 'is the man who really came to our rescue!' He raised his voice so that everyone could hear him. 'Ladies and gentlemen, I am delighted to be able to introduce Mr Archibald Davison, the famous archaeologist and author of numerous books on the Egypt of the Pharaohs and Ancient Greece.'

Colin couldn't help digging Peter in the ribs with his elbow. 'And an expert on Peruvian statues of Apollo and the Alexandrian pyramids!' he whispered slyly.

'I would like to add,' Mr Fitzwilliam went on, 'that Mr Davison gave his expert advice on the excavations entirely free of charge.'

Everyone in the Gallery clapped. Mr Davison just stood there rather stiffly, taking no notice of the clapping and the compliments.

Mr Fitzwilliam raised a hand, and the applause died down. Then he turned to point out something in the very middle of the room – a statue hidden by a sort of veil of white silk.

'And this really is the prize exhibit!' he said.

Those two little pests Susie and Binkie had come to the exhibition, of course, and they were standing as close to the statue as they could get, trying to lift the veil without being noticed so that they could see what it hid before anyone else!

'We have the Secret Seven to thank for this extra-ordinary discovery,' Mr Fitzwilliam was saying, 'and so I will ask them to unveil the statue.'

Feeling very excited, Janet stepped forward – she was the one who had actually *found* Fluvia, so the others all agreed that she ought to do the unveiling. She slowly pulled the silk veil off the statue.

'Fluvia!' announced Mr Fitzwilliam. 'Fluvia, our own local goddess from Romano-British times!'

There were cries of amazement and admiration, and then loud applause. Camera flashlights popped. Everyone was pressing close to the statue to get a good look at it, all talking at the same time and treading on each other's toes. The opening of the exhibition was a huge success!

In all the cheerful confusion, nobody noticed that Susie and Binkie were squabbling in a corner of the Gallery. Somehow they had got hold of the white silk veil, and now they were fighting over it!

'I had it first!' shouted Susie.

'No, you didn't! *I* did!' Binkie answered back.

'Let go, you beastly little thing! Susie shouted.

'Won't!' said Binkie.

The two little girls were tugging at the white silk with all their might, pulling so hard that they were both in danger of losing their balance. The tug-of-war went on for some time, but unfortunately nobody noticed. As they squabbled and tugged, Susie and Binkie were moving about the room, and soon they were close to the statue of Fluvia again.

'Let *go*, or I'll scratch your face!' Susie hissed between her teeth.

'*You* let go, or I'll cut your pigtails off! said silly Binkie.

The polished floor of the Gallery was quite slippery, and so they went sliding over it as they pulled the white silk. All of a sudden the pedestal with Fluvia standing on it was in between them. At that moment Binkie gave an extra hard pull – and Susie *did* lose her balance and swerve. The silk veil she was still holding caught on the pedestal and pulled it over!'

Crash!

The statue fell to the floor – and broke!

'Fluvia!' cried Pam, who was standing nearest.

'Fluvia!' gasped all the guests. They were horrified by what had happened.

'You little wretches!' growled Mr Fitzwilliam. He was holding Susie and Binkie by the scruffs of their necks. 'Have you any idea what that statue is worth?'

Janet was crying. Pam was crying. Barbara was crying. Peter was white with rage. Poor Jack didn't know where to look – one of the criminals was his own sister! George, who was standing beside him, was shaking all over. Colin was the only one of the Seven who kept calm And *he* was watching Archibald Davison. Mr Davison was taking advantage of all the confusion to make his way quietly to the door.

At that very moment the truth dawned!

'Why — the statue was only plaster!' somebody cried indignantly.

'Yes, so it was! Just plaster!' several other angry voices agreed.

'Trying to pull the wool over our eyes, eh?' asked the local chemist, who was known for his bad temper.

'I call it disgraceful!' said the doctor's wife. 'It ought not to be allowed!'

The Seven just couldn't make out what had happened. They stood rooted to the spot, looking at the broken bits of Fluvia lying on the floor. The three girls were so surprised that they stopped crying at once. Peter and Jack felt dreadful, with all the guests who had been invited to the opening of the exhibition accusing them of fraud!

'If these so-called Secret Seven are responsible they ought to be punished!' said the schoolmaster from the village angrily.

'And look at those "diamonds"! Nothing but paste!' said a large, fat woman.

'Mr Davison!' shouted Colin at the top of his voice. 'Mr Davison!'

Suddenly there was silence in the room. Colin ran to the window. Everyone else looked out too — and they saw the archaeologist jump into his Landrover outside the Hall, start up, and disappear down the gravel drive.

'We must catch him! Quick, follow me!' shouted

Peter to his friends, and he jumped out of the window as soon as Colin had got it open.

The rest of the Seven followed him, running as fast as they could, but of course it was no use. Even though the Landrover couldn't go very fast down the gravel drive, they had no chance of catching it up on foot. Peter, with great presence of mind, had jumped on the first bicycle he saw leaning against a wall, and pedalled away at top speed. He managed to keep the Landrover in sight as far as the big gates of the Hall – but once he was out on the road the archaeologist could speed up. Peter was just in time to see which way he turned, and then Archibald Davison was out of sight.

A little later the Secret Seven were holding an emergency meeting in the garden shed. They had been tricked – and they were not a bit pleased about it!

'I *did* tell you!' grumbled Colin, 'but you just wouldn't believe me! I *knew* he was an impostor. He *looked* like an impostor!'

'But that's just it, he didn't!' protested Barbara. 'He really did look awfully like the photographs of the real Archibald Davison!'

'Anyone who could grow a big beard like that could have made himself look like the real Archibald Davison.' Peter pointed out.

'Let's look at the situation calmly,' said Jack. 'There are two mysteries we've got to solve. One:

where is the *real* statue – the one we dug up? And two: where is the real Archibald Davison?'

'We've got no idea – and no hope of finding out either!' said Janet, gloomily.

'But why, *why* didn't we notice the statue was a fake?' asked George.

'*When* were the statues swapped – that's another question?' said Pam. 'And *how* did he manage to swap them?'

'I think he did it on the night of the storm,' said Colin. 'We all thought it was the wind that had broken that window, but it's much more likely that our friend Mr Davison broke it so as to get into the Gallery!'

'How about the copy of the statue, though?' asked George. 'Why didn't we notice that it *was* a copy?'

'If you think back,' Barbara pointed out, 'you'll remember that when we got to the Hall yesterday and saw the broken window, Fluvia was already underneath that white silk veil!'

'And none of us thought of lifting it to take a look!' said Pam sadly.

'It was a pretty good imitation, too,' added Jack.

'Yes, I don't suppose anyone would have noticed the deception if it hadn't been for your little sister and her friend Binkie,' agreed Peter. He got to his feet and said firmly, 'Well, we're not going to let that scoundrel get away with it! We must find it.'

'How? We might as well look for a needle in a haystack,' sighed Pam mournfully.

'No, we mightn't!' said Colin. 'Peter, you reached the gates at the end of the drive up to the Hall just before Mr Davison's Landrover was out of sight – which way did it go?'

'Oh, I see what you mean!' said Peter. 'He'd have had to turn right if he was going back through the village and on to the Manor Hotel for his things. Obviously he thought that would be too risky once the alarm was raised! No – he went left, as if he were going on along the road to Belling.'

'Then at least that gives us a bit of a lead,' said Colin. 'We needn't waste any time looking for him at his hotel. We can start straight off along the road to Belling ourselves!'

'Woof! Woof! Woof!, agreed Scamper, barking hard and leaping around as if he couldn't wait to be off.

'Scamper, why didn't we think of you before?' cried Janet. 'You'll help us, won't you?'

'I do believe that's exactly what he's trying to say!' said Barbara.

Everybody laughed – and suddenly the Secret Seven were feeling much more cheerful.

Five minutes later they were on their bicycles, pedalling along in single file towards Belling!

Chapter Eight

SCAMPER ON THE TRAIL

Scamper was running in front of the children, leading the way. They were well out of the village and on their way to Belling when he suddenly stopped by the side of the road.

'He's picked up the scent of something!' Peter told the others, signalling to them to stop too.

'Look – he's following a trail!' said Jack.

Sure enough, Scamper was going along beside the ditch with his nose down in the grass. All at once he stopped again.

What had he found? Nothing! Because next moment he shot off again without any warning. The Seven mounted their bicycles again and hurried after him. Quite soon they came to Marley Moor, the big stretch of moorland which lay between their own village and Belling. And here Scamper turned right off the road and started along a little footpath.

'I hope he's not just after rabbits!' said Peter, as the front wheel of his bicycle bumped over the rough grass and reached the footpath too.

The spaniel was still running ahead. 'Don't go so fast, Scamper!' begged Janet, who was trying to keep up with the others. She found it difficult to ride her cycle along the pebbly path, and all of a sudden the dog stopped beside a big puddle of water – just as if he had understood what his little mistress wanted.

'I expect he's thirsty after chasing along like that!' said Peter, getting off his bicycle.

'Oh, my word! Look at the path ahead of us!' said Colin, walking a little way on. 'It's a sea of mud!'

'That must be because of the storm the day before yesterday,' said Barbara.

The children sat down on some tuffets of grass to get their breath back. They didn't notice that Scamper wasn't drinking from his puddle after all.

The spaniel had picked up a scent! He put his nose to the ground and went snuffling all round the muddy path, searching to right and to left, doubling back on his own tracks, starting off again. All of a sudden he stopped and looked at the Seven. They were chattering away, paying him no attention!

'Woof! Woof!' he barked rather crossly. 'Woof! Woof!' He sounded as if he were saying, 'Come on, get up, you lazybones!'

Jack was the first to notice that the dog was trying to tell them something. 'What is it, Scamper?' he asked.

They all hurried over to the spot where the dog was waiting. 'I say, there are some tyre marks here!' exclaimed George.

'Yes – and quite new ones, too,' said Peter. 'I should say a car passed this way not long ago!'

'The Landrover!' cried Pam.

'Hold on!' said Colin cautiously. 'Tyre marks aren't actually proof like fingerprints, you know.'

'No, of course not,' agreed Barbara. 'But *you* know nobody much comes to Marley Moor. It's not a famous beauty spot, or anything like that. Look, it's the weekend, but there's no one in sight except us.'

'Yes, it does seem quite likely we're on the right track,' said Jack. 'Scamper, you're terrific!' he told the spaniel appreciatively. Scamper looked pleased!

Peter decided that they had better leave the bicycles behind, and go on following the path on foot.

In fact they had to leave the path quite often, because it was so muddy. The storm had left huge puddles behind.

However, the muddy state of the path meant that it was easy to follow the trail of the vehicle they were looking for! Its wheels had made quite deep furrows in some places. You could even see the Z-shaped patterns on the rubber of the tyres.

'Look – he must have had trouble here!' said Colin, pointing to some particularly deep tracks where the mud had been all churned up.

'Yes – he nearly got stuck!' said Peter. 'You can see that his wheels spun!'

'Oh, look – over there!' said Barbara, pointing. 'See those branches across the path?'

They all ran to look.

'And he *did* get stuck here!' said George happily. 'With all four wheels deep in the mud! He had to cover the path with branches so as to get going again!'

'That means he probably lost quite a lot of time,' said Barbara.

'In which case he may not be far off!' added Colin.

'Come on, Scamper – seek! Seek!' Peter cried.

And the spaniel set off again, with the Seven after him. But a little farther on they came out on a narrow road that went over the moor, and the path came to an end. So did their trail! The Landrover's tyres hadn't left any marks on the tarmac surface of the road.

'Oh, *blow*!' said Colin crossly. 'Blow and bother! Now we'll have to begin all over again.'

'I'm sure Scamper will be able to pick up the scent again,' Peter said. And he told Scamper to sniff all around the end of the path. But it was no good! Scamper did his best, but they had lost the archaeologist's trail, and there was nothing to be done about it!

It was lunch-time by now, and the children were hungry, but they didn't feel like going home. For one thing, they'd have to face Mr Fitzwilliam, and the Inspector from the police station – because by now the police would have been called in! So they decided to cut across the moor by a different way to pick up their bicycles, and then they would think what to do next.

They soon came to a little stream. In the usual way they would have stopped to paddle in it, but today, in spite of the heat, none of them jumped in after Scamper, who was splashing his way through the water, going upstream. It was nice and cool, and Scamper was enjoying himself. Tail wagging, he ran quite a long way ahead of the children, turned a corner and disappeared from sight. He seemed to be rather a long time coming back to them, and they were just getting a bit worried when they heard him barking in the distance. A little later they saw him chasing back towards them. They were surprised to see that after his bath in the stream, his lovely reddish-brown coat had gone a sort of grey!

'Goodness, Scamper, where *have* you been?' said Janet in surprise.

'He got wet through and then went and rolled in the dust!' said George, swerving away from Scamper as the dog gave himself a good shake!

'Well, go and rinse it off in the stream again!' Peter told the spaniel. 'We don't want a dirty dog with us!'

He was just taking Scamper over to the stream to wash him when Pam uttered an exclamation.

'I say! The water! Just look at the water!'

'It's gone all white!' said Colin in surprise.

'Well, it's not surprising Scamper lost the nice glossy shine on his coat,' said Peter, staring at the water.

'Someone must have thrown something into the stream – I wonder what?' said Barbara. 'What a shame – and it was such lovely, clear water, too! How thoughtless people can be!'

'Yes, we'll teach them not to go polluting a moorland stream!' said Peter. 'Come on, everyone – let's find out more about this!'

The Seven hurried along faster now. As they went further and further upstream, the water got thicker and whiter, until it looked like milk. They had to climb a slope, and soon they came to the source of the stream. The water flowed from a kind of little lake at the foot of a rock.

'There's nobody here!' said Jack in surprise. 'And nothing to explain what makes the water white, either!'

'We'd have to follow the stream underground to find out,' said Colin. 'Look – the water's already white when it flows out into the open here.'

'So we can't even solve *this* puzzle!' sighed Barbara. 'What a rotten day we're having.'

They all felt very disappointed. They were tired, too, and they sat down on the grass and stayed where they were for several minutes, just looking up at the sky. They were all thinking the same thing, and there was no need to put their thoughts into words! Where was the archaeologist? What had he done with the real statue? And would they ever find it again?

Well – they didn't find answers to any of those questions up in the clouds as they stared at the sky. No, the answers were much closer to hand, little as they were expecting them!

They suddenly heard a sound – the sound of footsteps. A man's footsteps!

Scamper's coat bristled. His nostrils were flaring. Peter went quietly up to the dog to make sure he didn't bark. The Seven exchanged glances in silence. They hardly dared to breathe as they lay flat on the ground. The footsteps went on for a little while, and then stopped.

'The sound comes from somewhere higher up this slope!' Peter whispered. 'Whoever polluted the stream must be up there.'

'Come on, then!' Jack whispered back.

Following Peter, the Seven all rose to their feet quietly and climbed on up the slope, rounding the big rock which had been hiding them and whoever the footsteps belonged to from each other. They hadn't gone very far when they stopped and stared in astonishment.

There was Mr Davison's Landrover, parked outside the mouth of a cave only a few paces away from them!

Nobody said a word, but their eyes were shining! They had caught up with Archibald Davison after all! They took what cover they could find and waited

for the archaeologist to appear – and they didn't have to wait long, either.

He came out of the cave with his arms full of tools and implements, and put them in the Landrover. This had obviously been his hideout, and his hotel room was only for show, to make him look respectable!

Just then Scamper nearly spoiled everything – he jumped up in the air twice, trying to catch a butterfly. But Peter instinctively tackled him and brought him down, just as if they were playing rugger. Luckily the spaniel didn't bark, and the archaeologist's back happened to be turned at that moment. Davison went into the cave again. He hadn't noticed anything.

Peter wasted no more time. The others watched in surprise as he made for the Landrover with his penknife in his hand. It was the work of a moment to slash all four tyres and take the ignition keys out of the vehicle.

'Come on!' he whispered, beckoning to the other children. They came out of the bushes where they had been hiding and hurried over to him. 'We're going in to find out just what that scoundrel is up to!' he told them in a low voice. There was a torch lying in the Landrover, and he picked that up too. 'But we must be careful,' he added. 'Everybody keep together.'

The girls were feeling rather alarmed as they slipped quietly into the cave. It was long and narrow, and seemed to go straight into the hill, like a corridor. The light faded away as the children went further in

They turned a sharply angled corner, and found themselves in pitch darkness. Jack, who was bringing up the rear of the little procession, picked Scamper up, and then they all held hands so as to keep in touch. They went on. They had to grope through the dark – Peter wasn't using the torch, for fear of attracting the archaeologist's attention. They went about thirty metres in complete silence. Where *was* Archibald Davison?

Colin, for one, was just beginning to suspect something when they heard the archaeologist's voice behind them!

'Too late, my dear children!' he said mockingly, flashing the blinding light of a torch in their eyes. 'I've got you now – you walked straight into my trap!' And his loud laughter echoed all round the cave!

Chapter Nine

IN THE CAVE

The children's teeth were chattering with fright! They were terrified. Davison stood between them and their way of escape. They were his prisoners!

All the same, Peter had enough presence of mind to switch on the torch he was carrying himself. He saw the archaeologist standing in the middle of the tunnel along which they had come – and he was holding the golden statue.

'Another time you'd better remember that people can see things in a rear-view mirror!' he said triumphantly. 'You should have tied up that dog of yours.'

He swept the beam of his torch over the Seven, enjoying the sight of their terror.

'You're too inquisitive!' he went on. 'I've had to change my plans, all because of you. Still, that may not be a bad thing!' And he stopped to laugh out loud again. 'I'm going to leave you where I planned to leave the statue!' he told the children. 'I was going to hide it here until the hue and cry had died down. Well, that's just too bad so far as you're concerned!'

He waved the beam of the torch round the cave, so that the Seven could see where they were. They had come out into a huge, underground room without noticing it as they walked along the dark.

'You'll have plenty of time to sit and feel sorry you ever poked your nose into other people's business!' said the archaeologist. 'There's room for all of you — and I expect the air will last about a fortnight! But unless some miracle . . .'

He didn't finish what he had been going to say — he didn't need to! Scamper was howling miserably, and that made the archaeologist laugh again. The Seven were rooted to the ground. They stared at him.

'Well, goodbye, children!' he said. 'And good luck!'

And he suddenly kicked away a big wooden wedge that nobody had noticed before. Several tons of rocks tumbled down from another tunnel running into the hillside above the main one. The only way out of the cave was blocked!

The Seven had instinctively jumped back, but as the thunderous noise of the rock-fall died away into echoes, they felt they were choking. The rocks had raised clouds of dust as they fell. You couldn't see a thing, and it was almost impossible to breathe.

'Golly — we're in a tight spot now!' muttered Peter.

'He'd fixed that mechanism up to block the cave!' whispered Jack. 'What a horrible thing to think of!'

George wasn't feeling at all well – he couldn't seem to get his breath back.

'We'd better go further into the cave, or we'll choke,' said Colin.

They took refuge at the far end of the huge underground room and waited for the dust to settle, breathing through their handkerchiefs. Most of it had fallen to the ground again after about fifteen minutes, and they could see each other by the light of the torch. What a sight they were! They looked like white-faced clowns, with staring eyes and their hair full of powdery dust! Everybody was shedding tears, even the boys – the dust had got into their eyes too, and they couldn't help it.

'This really *is* a tight spot!' Peter kept saying.

Poor Scamper had buried his head in his forepaws and was 'playing dead'.

'Here, give me that torch, Peter!' said Colin, pulling himself together. 'We can't stay here, and the sooner we get out the better!'

'You're right, Colin,' Jack agreed. 'We're going to make our escape!'

'But how?' sobbed poor little Janet. '*How*?'

'Well, I don't know yet,' said Colin, 'but we're jolly well not going to rot away in this cave!'

He took a good look round it. The huge room was almost circular. It was very wide, and the roof looked a very long way up. There was that great pile of fallen rocks blocking the tunnel along which they had come – but there was another tunnel too, on the far side of the cave! A narrow one which seemed to go down a gentle slope.

'There's our emergency exit!' said Colin, trying to sound cheerful. 'Mind you don't bump your heads – the ceiling's rather low.'

The children set off along the narrow tunnel, but they hadn't gone far before they heard a strange sound. They all stopped to listen.

'What do you think it is?' asked Colin.

'Sounds like water!' said Jack.

'Running water – a river!' Peter guessed.

They quickened their pace, and soon they came out of the tunnel. There was a big fault in the rock here, and a stream was flowing through it.

'It must come out somewhere,' said Colin. 'Let's follow it!'

The Seven were beginning to feel a little more hopeful now. Even Scamper had stopped trembling.

They followed the stream, which had cut itself a channel through the rock, and when they rounded a bend they were surprised to see two large, opened bags of plaster standing on the rocky bank!

'Look at that!' said Peter. 'The water's turning white where it laps against those bags of plaster!'

'That must mean this is the same stream we were following just now out in the open!' said Barbara.

'We're going to be all right!' said Colin happily.

'I say – did you see that? Someone's left some empty folders lying about!' said George, pointing to the ground.

Barbara picked one up and read what it said on the cover. 'Gold Leaf.'

'Gold leaf?' asked Janet in surprise. 'Whatever is that?'

'It's very, very thin sheets of gold,' Jack told her. 'Artists use it, and so do confectioners sometimes. They put it on very grand, special chocolates to make them look golden.'

'Well!' said Colin. 'So this is where Mr Davison made the fake statue! He mixed up the plaster and moulded it into shape, and then he covered it with gold leaf!'

They found some empty gas canisters, too – obviously the archaeologist had been using them for lighting. Then the children found a lot of little lead ball bearings. Whatever could *they* have been for?

Barbara guessed the answer to that question!

'Plaster's light – but lead is heavy!' she said. 'I expect he was using these lead ball bearings to give his plaster mixture extra weight, so that the statue would seem to be made of gold!'

'Peter whistled appreciatively. 'Well done, Sherlock Holmes! Now, where's the way out? We must hurry – we have plenty of evidence against Archibald Davison now!'

The children went on following the white waters of the stream, but not much further on it flowed into a little lake. 'Oh dear – the stream ends here!' said Colin, feeling very disappointed after all his high hopes

'And so does the tunnel!' said Peter gloomily.

Sure enough, the tunnel through which the stream had been running came to a dead end. The little lake was surrounded by walls of rock.

'We shouldn't have counted our chickens before they were hatched,' said Pam unhappily.

'Yes – Davison must have known we'd find this tunnel, but he also knew it wouldn't lead us out into the open!' George said. 'We really are prisoners here!'

'We'll see about that!' said Colin. His blood was really up now. Watched by his surprised friends, he took off his shirt, jeans and shoes. 'We'll see about that!' he repeated – and he dived into the milky water!

The others expected him to come up a little later, but he didn't. The surface of the water was perfectly smooth.

'What's he doing?' asked Janet anxiously.

Nobody replied. All eyes were turned to the surface of the lake.

Several seconds passed by. Soon Colin had been down below for a full minute. 'Oh, my goodness, suppose something's happened to him?' whispered Pam, sobbing.

Peter was feeling very worried indeed as he counted seconds in his head.

'Ninety-two, ninety-three, ninety-four . . .' After three minutes he stopped. 'He must be drowned!' he said in an expressionless voice.

But just then bubbles broke on the surface of the water.

'He's coming up!' shouted George.

However, the first thing that came up, a moment later, was a large ox-eye daisy! It was followed by Colin's hand, and then Colin's smiling face. He was looking very happy indeed.

'There's a way through to the outside!' he told his friends. 'Look – I got right out into the open and picked this flower to prove it!'

'Hurrah!' cried the others. 'Well done, Colin!'

And Scamper danced a jig on the banks of the lake!

Peter was already taking his clothes off, and so were Jack and Barbara. They all three dived into the water, following Colin's lead. He showed them the way out he had found.

They let themselves sink right to the bottom of the

little lake. The odd thing was that the lower they sank, the brighter the water seemed! When they reached the very bottom Colin wriggled underneath a rock. The other three followed him – and suddenly they found they could kick out and rise to the surface again. They were out in the open! When they had got their breath back, they saw that the sun was shining in the sky above. They were back at the place where they had found the source of the hillside stream and heard the archaeologists footsteps above them!

Without wasting a moment, they jumped out of the water and ran back to the mouth of the cave. The Landrover, with its flat tyres, was still standing there. They looked in its toolbox and found some ropes, pickaxes and iron bars as well as the usual tools – all the stuff the archaeologist had had to leave behind him!

'Quick!' said Peter. 'We must get the others out. Janet can't come the way we did, she hates putting her head under water – and Pam doesn't much like it either.'

'And George couldn't stay under all that time – you know he gets asthma,' said Barbara.

'And don't forget dear old Scamper!' added Jack

'Well, come on, we've got all we need here!' said Colin. 'I even found a spare torch in the Landrover.'

They went back into the cave and down the tunnel as far as the fallen rocks. 'It's all right, you three!' called Peter. 'Here we come!'

Chapter Ten

THE IMPOSTOR IS CAUGHT!

'Oh, thank goodness! You're all right!' said Pam's voice on the other side of the heap of rocks.

Jack was in luck – he managed to find a crack among the rocks, big enough for him to pass several pickaxes through it one by one. He pushed through the end of a rope too. The rope was long enough to reach from the cave to the Landrover at the other end of the tunnel.

George, Pam and Janet roped the pickaxes firmly together and got them into place, so that when the rope was pulled, they would push against the rocks from inside the cave. 'Ready!' said George, after a while.

'Right – now go to the far end of the cave,' Peter told them. 'We'll pull on the rope from outside.'

He, Colin, Jack and Barbara went back into the open, and he got behind the wheel of the Landrover. Jack tied their end of the rope firmly to its bumper, and Peter took the ignition keys he had removed from the Landrover out of his pocket and turned the engine on. What a good thing he was used to driving his father's tractor in the fields! He put his foot on the accelerator pedal, and the rope stretched tight.

However, he could hardly move the vehicle at all. The rope was taut, and he didn't want to break it, but the wall of rocks at the other end of it didn't seem as if it was going to give way.

Peter tried accelerating again, but the wheels of the Landrover began to spin dangerously. Colin and Jack came to give a good push, and all of a sudden they heard a loud crash inside the tunnel. Some of the rocks had shifted. They could tell, because the Landrover had moved at least a metre. Peter switched the engine off and jumped out to see what had happened. But as he started along the tunnel, Scamper came dashing out to meet him, followed by George and the two girls.

Everyone shouted for joy, and they all danced around and hugged each other! Then Colin, Peter, Jack and Barbara went back for their clothes.

The next thing was to catch up with Archibald Davison again, and as soon as possible.

'He can't be very far away,' said Jack. 'He's on foot, carrying that heavy golden statue. He won't be able to go very fast.'

They were about to set off the same way as they had come, but Peter called them back. 'Here, we've got a vehicle we can use for once, so let's use it!' he said. 'Everyone get in!'

'But —' said Pam.

'Don't worry,' Peter told her. 'It's no harder to drive one of these than my father's tractor on the farm – and we *can't* go very fast with four flat tyres!'

So at last Pam consented to join the others in the Landrover, and Peter started it up again. The engine coughed and spluttered once or twice, but then it began to turn over quite smoothly, and Peter drove the Landrover away from the cave.

Janet, George, Jack and Colin, who were in the back, were bumped and jolted about, and they had to hold tight to keep their balance. The ground wasn't exactly as smooth as a good main road, and the flat tyres didn't help either. Peter clutched the steering wheel very tight as the Landrover lurched to and fro. From a distance you would have wondered who could be driving in such a wobbly line!

Luckily they quite soon got back to the road, and now the going was easier. Peter was even able to accelerate a little. He knew he wasn't supposed to drive on a road, at his age, but he just hoped that if they caught Davison, his friend the Inspector would turn a blind eye!

Colin stood up in the back, with the others hanging on to him for safety's sake, so that he could get a good view of the country round them. He felt rather like a lookout up in the crow's-nest at the top of a ship's mast – and in fact he suddenly shouted out, 'I say! Shipwreck to port! There's Davison! Go on, Peter – that way!'

And Peter drove the Landrover after its owner!

Archibald Davison seemed to be exhausted and out of breath. The Seven could see he was tiring. He had realised that they were after him, and was running as hard as he could. Suppose he managed to run off the road and escape from them by hiding somewhere? The Seven never took their eyes off him. Luckily the moor was very flat and open, and didn't offer much in the way of a hiding place.

Peter tried going faster, but it was no use – the Landrover started to go into a skid. 'Never mind,' he said, slowing down again. 'We'll soon catch him. He must be nearly tired out!'

'This is a real hunt!' said Barbara. She was enjoying herself.

Gradually they were gaining ground on Davison. He kept turning to look behind him, and the Seven could see the alarm on his face. He was defeated now, and he knew it! The hunt was going to end in his capture!

The Landrover came closer and closer. Soon it was right on his heels. Then Colin had a brilliant idea.

'I know what!' he said, going down on the floor of the Landrover to find the rope they had used just now to pull down the wall of fallen rocks. He tied a good firm knot in it. 'We'll lasso him!' And he stood up and threw his lasso. 'Oh, bother! Missed!' he said, laughing, and he pulled in the rope for another try.

'Go on!' said Jack. 'You'll get him next time!'

Colin's lasso whistled through the air once more and landed close to the archaeologist, stinging his

cheek.

'Can you go on a *little* bit closer, Peter?' Colin asked his friend.

'Hold on, everyone, I'll try!' said Peter. The Land-rover swerved rather alarmingly as he ventured to put his foot down just a little bit – but now they were three precious metres nearer to Davison.

'That should do the trick!' said Colin, whirling his lasso in the air above his head. Whoosh! The rope flew through the air again – and this time the looped end fell neatly round Archibald Davison.

'Real Wild West stuff!' said Jack, clapping.

'Come on, give me a hand!' Colin yelled to the others, and they all hauled on the rope. It tightened around the archaeologist, pinning his arms to his body. Peter slowed down enough for him to be able to follow the Landrover on foot, and George seized his chance to get out and grab the golden statue. He put it down on the front seat of the Landrover beside Pam and Barbara.

Peter turned down the road to their own village. Passing motorists were astonished to see a Landrover steering such a wobbly course – and when they came closer they were even more surprised to see that it was full of children, and was followed by a man tied up, on foot, and looking like a real gallows-bird of the old days!

The village came into sight just as Pam saw that there was a radio in the Landrover, and suggested turning it on. 'We might come home in triumph to the sound of music!' she said, smiling.

Sure enough, when they switched the radio on they got a very cheerful tune which they already knew. They all started singing to it in chorus. Archibald Davison wasn't singing as he walked gloomily behind them, though! Scamper was running along beside him, baring his teeth. A few moments later the music on the radio stopped, and the children heard a voice reading the news. They didn't take much notice – but then suddenly they heard the newsreader announce something that they *did* find interesting.

'The famous archaeologist Archibald Davison was found this morning in the cellar of his own country house. He had been a prisoner there for nearly three months. Mr Davison's attacker, a man by the name of Anthony Bertram, had locked him in the cellar with adequate supplies of food and bottled water for a long period. It seems extraordinary that a man could be kept a prisoner against his will, and unknown to anyone, in this day and age. However, Mr Davison's house lies in a remote part of the country, and his neighbours believed he was away on an expedition to Peru. It was only when some men laying cables came close enough to hear his shouts that the archaeologist was found. Bertram, Mr Davison's former assistant, has worked for a number of years producing copies of antiquities for the British Museum. Acquaintances say he appears to be perfectly sane, and it is hard to guess at his reasons for attacking the eminent archaeologist. He has disappeared and the police have been alerted to look out for him. It is hoped that he will soon be brought to justice, but at the moment Anthony Bertram is still on the run.'

Peter switched the radio off. The children all looked at each other, stunned.

'So I was right all along!' said Colin. 'I *knew* he wasn't the real Davison!'

'How awful!' said Barbara angrily. 'He must have come here to find Fluvia and steal her. 'That was what he meant to do from the start!'

'Yes — but he didn't know he'd have *us* to deal with!' said Jack proudly.

Pam, sitting in the back of the Landrover, couldn't take her eyes off Anthony Bertram, alias Archibald Davison.

'A fake archaeologist!' she said to herself, trying to take it in. 'Well, whatever the radio news said, he's *not* on the run any more!'

Ten minutes later, the Seven arrived at the police station with their prisoner.

There was quite a crowd to meet them! Everyone had heard the story of the fake Roman statue by now. Mr Fitzwilliam was down at the police station himself, talking to the Inspector, when the Land-rover drove up.

'Goodness me, it's the Seven!' he cried, when he saw Peter sitting at the wheel. Then he saw the children's prisoner tied to the bumper and walking along behind. 'What on earth have you young people been doing?' he asked, puzzled.

'We've come to hand a criminal over to the police,' said Peter proudly.

'And here's the *real* statue of Fluvia!' Jack added,

giving the Inspector the golden statue.

'This man's real name is Anthony Bertram,' Colin explained. 'And he imprisoned the archaeologist Archibald Davison in his own house – the poor man's only just been found! Then he pretended to be Mr Davison himself, and came here so that he could steal the statue.'

The Inspector and Mr Fitzwilliam looked from one to other of the Seven. They hadn't been listening to the radio news, so they had no idea what Colin was talking about! Both of them were very puzzled. Peter had to explain the whole story in detail.

Meanwhile Pam got close to the impostor, stood right in front of him and looked hard at his face. Bertram pretended to take no notice.

After several seconds, Pam could bear it no longer. She simply *had* to know! She put out both hands, grabbed the man's beard and tugged hard. He yelled with pain!

Pam went back to the others. She looked rather disappointed – and she had a tuft of hair in her hand.

'I couldn't help wondering!' she said. 'But it wasn't a false beard after all!'

A complete list of new adventures about the SECRET SEVEN

---

1. THE SEVEN AND THE LION HUNT
2. THE SEVEN GO HAUNTING
3. THE SEVEN AND THE MAGICIAN
4. THE SEVEN STRIKE GOLD
5. THE SEVEN TO THE RESCUE

A complete list of the SECRET SEVEN ADVENTURES by Enid Blyton

KNIGHT BOOKS